For Alice Mary Hathway
J. W.

For Paul and Denise
J. F.

Text copyright © 2008 by Jeanne Willis   Illustrations copyright © 2008 by Jan Fearnley

ISBN 978-0-7636-3470-4

Printed in Mexico

This book was typeset in Stempel Schneider. The illustrations were done in watercolor and ink.

Candlewick Press, 2067 Massachusetts Avenue, Cambridge, Massachusetts 02140

Mommy, Do You Love Me?

JEANNE WILLIS

illustrated by JAN FEARNLEY

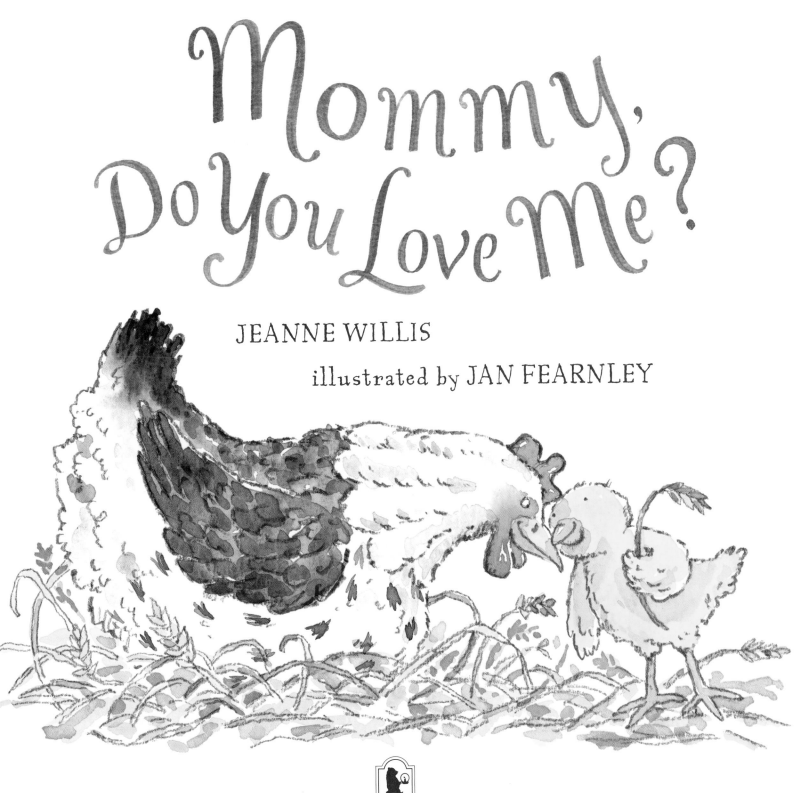

CANDLEWICK PRESS

CAMBRIDGE, MASSACHUSETTS

"Mommy, do you love me?"
asked Little Chick.

"I love you more than words can
ever say," said his mommy.

And she gave him a peck
on the cheek.

"But will you always love me,
even if I look like this?" he cheeped, and he
made a funny face.

"Yes!" she said. "You'll always be beautiful
to me."

Just to make sure, Little Chick
found the muddiest puddle
on the farm—

and jumped in it.

When he came back, he was
covered from head to tail in muck.
"Mommy," he said, "do you *still* love me,
even when I'm muddy?"

"Yes," she said. "You're *still* my
sweet Little Chick underneath."

And she made him all
fluffy again.

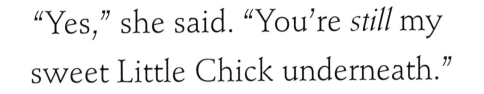

Just then, Little Chick's friends came over.
They had a race.

Little Chick didn't win.

"Mommy," he said, "do you *still* love me, even though I came in last place?"
"Yes," said his mommy. "You always come in first place with me."

And she gave him a red rose.
Little Chick ran to show his friends.
"Your mommy must *really* love you!"
they said.

But on
the way
home,

he dropped the rose . . .

and
all
the
petals
fell
off.

"Mommy," he cheeped, "do you *still* love me,
even though I ruined my rose?"
"Yes," she said. "Roses don't last long, but
my love for you will last forever."

And she put her wing around him.

Little Chick was so happy to be loved
that he cheeped and he chirped
and he crowed . . .

very, very loudly.

"Please be quiet,"
said his mommy.

But Little Chick
wouldn't.

He shrieked and screeched
and squawked even
louder.

His mommy tried again.
"*Please* be quiet,
Little Chick."

But Little Chick wouldn't listen. He just kept shouting

louder and **louder.**

So his mommy shouted back . . .

PLEASE
BE
QUIET,
LITTLE
CHICK!

Little Chick
couldn't believe his ears—
his mommy had shouted at him!

Didn't she love him anymore?

He was so upset that he ran away and hid his head under his wing.

His mommy came looking for him. "What's wrong, Little Chick?" she said. "Mommy," he cried, "do you *still* love me, even when I'm bad?" "Little Chick," she said, "sometimes you make me mad, and sometimes you make me sad, but no matter what you say or do, I will always love you."

"Why?" asked Little Chick. "Because I'm your mommy," she said.

"I love you, too," he said.

"Ah," said his mommy. "But will you always love me, even if I look like this?"

And she made a funny face.

Little Chick laughed and laughed.
"Mommy," he said, "sometimes you make
me mad, and sometimes you make me sad,
but no matter what you say or do,
I will always love you."

"Why?" asked his mommy.

"Because I'm your Little Chick!"
he said.